Defoe
Abbott
Marx
Hardy
Melville
Montaigne
Machiavelli
Haggard
Chesterton
Cooper
Emerson
Joyce
Austen
Hugo
Eliot
Grimm
Carroll
Christie
Stoker
Wilde
Maupassant
Byron
Molière
Schiller
Garnett
Einstein
Fitzgerald
Engels
Smith
Kafka
Goethe
Hawthorne
Hall
Cotton
Dostoyevsky
Willis
Baum
Kipling
Doyle
Henry
Nietzsche
Leslie
Dumas
Flaubert
Turgenev
Balzac
Stockton
Vatsyayana
Crane
Burroughs
Verne
Curtis
Tocqueville
Gogol
Vinci
Homer
Widger
Tolstoy
Whitman
Busch
Darwin
Thoreau
Potter
Freud
Zola
Twain
Scott
Plato
Harte
Kant
Jowett
Stevenson
Dickens
Burton
Hesse
Andersen
Cervantes
London
Descartes
Voltaire
Poe
Aristotle
Wells
Hale
James
Hastings
Cooke
Bunner
Shakespeare
Richter
Chambers
Irving
Doré
Dante
Chekhov
da
Shaw
Wodehouse
Benedict
Alcott
Swift
Pushkin
Newton

AF303443

 tredition®

tredition was established in 2006 by Sandra Latusseck and Soenke Schulz. Based in Hamburg, Germany, tredition offers publishing solutions to authors and publishing houses, combined with worldwide distribution of printed and digital book content. tredition is uniquely positioned to enable authors and publishing houses to create books on their own terms and without conventional manufacturing risks.

For more information please visit: www.tredition.com

TREDITION CLASSICS

This book is part of the TREDITION CLASSICS series. The creators of this series are united by passion for literature and driven by the intention of making all public domain books available in printed format again - worldwide. Most TREDITION CLASSICS titles have been out of print and off the bookstore shelves for decades. At tredition we believe that a great book never goes out of style and that its value is eternal. Several mostly non-profit literature projects provide content to tredition. To support their good work, tredition donates a portion of the proceeds from each sold copy. As a reader of a TREDITION CLASSICS book, you support our mission to save many of the amazing works of world literature from oblivion. See all available books at www.tredition.com.

Project Gutenberg

The content for this book has been graciously provided by Project Gutenberg. Project Gutenberg is a non-profit organization founded by Michael Hart in 1971 at the University of Illinois. The mission of Project Gutenberg is simple: To encourage the creation and distribution of eBooks. Project Gutenberg is the first and largest collection of public domain eBooks.

The Water goats and other troubles

Ellis Parker Butler

Imprint

This book is part of TREDITION CLASSICS

Author: Ellis Parker Butler
Cover design: Buchgut, Berlin – Germany

Publisher: tredition GmbH, Hamburg - Germany
ISBN: 978-3-8424-2413-5

www.tredition.com
www.tredition.de

By Ellis Parker Butler

By The Same Author

Pigs is Pigs The Great American Pie Company Mike Flannery
On Duty and off The Thin Santa Claus That Pup, Kilo, etc.

Contents

THE WATER GOATS AND OTHER TROUBLES

I. THE WATER GOATS

"And then," said the landscape gardener, combing his silky, pointed beard gently with his long, artistic fingers, "in the lake you might have a couple of gondolas. Two would be sufficient for a lake of this size; amply sufficient. Yes," he said firmly, "I would certainly advise gondolas. They look well, and the children like to ride on them. And so do the adults. I would have two gondolas in the lake."

Mayor Dugan and the City Council, meeting as a committee of the whole to receive the report of the landscape gardener and his plan for the new public park, nodded their heads sagely.

"Sure!" said Mayor Dugan. "We want two of thim — of thim gon — thim gon — "

"Gondolas," said the landscape gardener. "Sure!" said Mayor Dugan, "we want two of thim. Remimber th' gondolas, Toole."

"I have thim fast in me mind," said Toole. "I will not let thim git away, Dugan."

The landscape gardener stood a minute in deep thought, looking at the ceiling.

"Yes, that is all!" he said. "My report, and the plan, and what I have mentioned, will be all you need."

Then he shook hands with the mayor and with all the city councilmen and left Jeffersonville forever, going back to New York where landscape gardeners grow, and the doors were opened and the committee of the whole became once more the regular meeting of the City Council.

The appropriation for the new park was rushed through in twenty minutes, passing the second and third readings by the reading of the title under a suspension of the by-laws, and being unanimously adopted. It was a matter of life and death with Mayor Dugan and his ring. Jeffersonville was getting tired of the joyful grafters, and murmurs of discontent were concentrating into threats of a reform party to turn the cheerful rascals out. The new park was to be a sop thrown to the populace — something to make the city proud of itself and grateful to its mayor and council. It was more than a pet scheme of Mayor Dugan, it was a lifeboat for the ring. In half an hour the committees had been appointed, and the mayor turned to the regular business. Then from his seat at the left of the last row little Alderman Toole arose.

"Misther Mayor," he said, "how about thim—thim don—thim don—Golas!" whispered Alderman Grevemeyer hoarsely, "dongolas."

"How about thim dongolas, Misther Mayor?" asked Alderman Toole.

"Sure!" said the mayor. "Will annyone move that we git two dongolas t' put in th' lake for th' kids t' ride on? Will annyone move that Alderman Toole be a conmittee of wan t' git two dongolas t' put in th' lake?"

"I make dot motions," said Alderman Greveneyer, half raising his great bulk from his seat and sinking back with a grunt.

"Sicond th' motion," said Alderman Toole.

"Moved and siconded," said the mayor, "that Alderman Toole be a committee t' buy two dongolas t' put in th' lake for th' kids t' ride on. Ye have heard th' motion."

The motion was unanimously carried. That was the kind of City Council Mayor Dugan had chosen.

When little Alderman Toole dropped into Casey's saloon that night on his way home he did not slip meekly to the far end of the bar, as he usually did. For the first time in his aldermanic career he had been put on a committee where he would really have something to do, and he felt the honour. He boldly took a place between the big mayor and Alderman Grevemeyer, and said: "One of th' same, Casey," with the air of a man who has matters of importance on his mind. He felt that things were coming his way. Even the big mayor seemed to appreciate it, for he put his hand affectionately on Toole's shoulder.

"Mike," said the mayor, "about thim dongolas, now; have ye thought anny about where ye would be gettin' thim?"

"I have not," said Toole. "I was thinkin' 'twould be good t' think it over a bit, Dugan. Mebby 'twould be best t' git thim at Chicagy." He looked anxiously at the mayor's face, hoping for some sign of approval or disapproval, but the mayor's face was noncommittal. "But mebby it wouldn't," concluded Toole. As a feeler he added: "Would ye be wantin' me t' have thim made here, Dugan?"

The big mayor patted Toole on the shoulder indulgently.

"It's up t' you, Mike," he said. "Ye know th' way Dugan does things, an' th' way he likes thim done. I trust thim that I kin trust, an' whin I put a man on committee I'm done wid th' thing. Of coorse," he added, putting his mouth close to Toole's ear, and winking at Grevemeyer, "ye will see that there is a rake-off for me an' th' byes."

"Sure!" said Toole.

The big mayor turned back to the bar and took a drink from his glass. Grevemeyer took a drink from his glass, also. So did Toole, gravely. Dugan wiped his mouth on the back of his hand and turned to Toole again.

"Mike," he said, "what do ye think? Mebby 'twould do as well t' git a couple of sicond-hand dongolas an' have thim painted up. If they was in purty good shape no wan would know th' difference, an' 'twould make a bit more rake-off fer th' byes, mebby."

"Th' same word was on th' ind o' me tongue, Dugan," said Toole, nodding his head slowly. "I was considerin' this very minute where I could lay me hand on a couple of purty good dongolas that has not been used much. Flannagan could paint thim up fine!"

"Or Stoltzenau could do such paintings," interposed Grevemeyer.

"Sure!" agreed the big mayor. He toyed with his glass a moment. "Mike," he said suddenly, "what th' divil is a dongola, anyhow?"

Mike Toole was just raising his glass to his lips with the movements of one accustomed to hold conversation with the mayor. His left hand rested on his hip, with his arm akimbo, and his hat was tipped carelessly to the back of his head. The hand raising his glass stopped short where it was when he heard the mayor's question. He frowned at the glass—scowled at it angrily.

"A dongola, Dugan"—he said slowly, and stopped. "A dongola"—he repeated. "A dongola—did ye ask me what a dongola might be, Dugan?"

The big mayor nodded, and Grevemeyer leaned forward to catch the answer. Casey, too, leaned on his bar and listened. Alderman Toole raised his glass to his lips and filled his mouth with the liquor. Instantly he dashed the glass furiously to the floor. He jerked off his hat and cast it into a far corner and pulled off his coat, throwing it after his hat. He was climbing on to the bar when the big mayor and Grevemeyer laid their hands on the little man and held him tightly. The big mayor shook him once and set him on the floor.

"Mike!" said the big mayor. "What's th' matter wid ye? What are ye goin' afther Casey that way for? Is it crazy ye are? Or have ye gone insane?"

"Knock-out drops!" shouted Toole, shaking his fist at Casey, who looked down at him in astonishment. "Knock-out drops! I will have th' law on ye, Casey. I will have th' joint closed! I'll teach ye t' be givin' knock-out drops t' th' aldermin of th' city!"

"Mike!" cried the big mayor, giving him another vigorous shake. "Shut up wid ye! Casey wouldn't be givin' ye annything that wasn't good for ye. Casey wouldn't be givin' ye knock-out drops."

"No?" whispered Mike angrily. "No? Wouldn't he, Dugan? An' what has he done t' me mimory, then, Dugan? What has he put in th' drink t' rob me of me mimory? Wan minute ago I knew as well anny other man what a dongola is like, an' now I have no mimory of anny dongolas at all. Wan minute ago I could have told ye th' whole history of dongolas, from th' time of Adam up till now, an' have drawed a picture of wan that annywan could recognize—an' now I wouldn't know wan if ye was show it t' me! I was about t' tell ye th' whole history of dongolas, Dugan; 'twas on th' ind of me tongue t' give ye a talk on dongolas, whin I took a drink. Ye saw me take a drink, Grevemeyer?"

"Ya!" said Grevemeyer, nodding his head solemnly. "You took such a drink!"

"Sure," said Toole, arranging his vest. "Grevemeyer saw me take th' drink—an now I have no mimory of dongolas at all. If ye was t' show me a chromo of wan I wouldn't know was it a dongola or what. I'm ashamed of ye, Casey!"

"If ye done it, Casey, ye hadn't have ought t' have done it," said Dugan reprovingly. "Th' mind of him might be ruined intirely."

"Stop, Dugan!" said Toole hastily. "I forgive him. Me mind will likely be all right by mornin'. 'Tis purty good yit, ixcipt on th' subject of dongolas. I'm timporarily out of remimbrance what dongolas is. 'Tis odd how thim knock-out drops works, Grevemeyer."

"Ya!" said the alderman unsuspectingly, "gifing such a forgetfulness on such easy things as dongolas."

"Sure! You tell Dugan what dongolas is, Grevemeyer," said Toole quickly.

Grevemeyer looked at his glass thoughtfully. His mind worked slowly always, but he saw that it would not do for him to have knock-out drops so soon after Toole.

"Ach!" he exclaimed angrily. "You are insulting to me mit such questions Toole. So much will I tell you—never ask Germans what is dongolas. It is not for Germans to talk about such things. Ask Casey."

Casey scratched his head thoughtfully.

"Dongolas?" he repeated. "I have heard th' word, Grevemeyer. Wait a bit! 'Tis something about shoes. Sure! I remimber, now! 'Twas dongola shoes wan of me kids had, last winter, an' no good they were, too. Dongolas is shoes, Grevemeyer—laced shoes— dongolas is laced shoes."

The big mayor leaned his head far back and laughed long and loud. He pounded on the bar with his fist, and slapped Toole on the back.

"Laced shoes!" he cried, wiping his eyes, and then he became suddenly serious. "'Twould not be shoes, Casey," he said gravely. "Thim dongolas was ricomminded by th' landscape-gardener from New Yorrk. 'Twould not be sinsible t' ricommind us put a pair of laced shoes in th' park lake fer th' kids t' ride on."

"'Twould not seem so," said Toole, shaking his head wisely. "I wisht me mind was like it always is. 'Tis a pity—"

"Stop!" cried Casey. "I have it! Thim was kid shoes. Thim dongolas was kid shoes."

"So said, Casey," said Duo'an "For th' kid."

"No," said Casey, "of th' kid."

"Sure!" said Gravemeyer. "So it is—the shoes of the child."

"Right fer ye!" exclaimed Casey. "Th' kid shoes of th' kid. 'Twas kid leather they were made out of, Dugan. Th' dongola is some fancy kind of a goat. Like box-calf is th' skin of th' calf of th' box-cow. Th' dongola is some foreign kind of a goat, Dugan."

"Ho, ho-o-o!" cried Toole, suddenly, knocking on his forehead with the knuckles of his fist. The three men turned their eyes upon him and stared.

"What ails ye now, Mike?" asked Dugan, disgustedly.

"Ho-o-o!" he cried again, slapping himself on the top of his head. "Me mind is comm' back t' me, Dugan! Th' effects of th' knock-out drops is wearin' off! I recall now that th' dongola is some fancy kind of a goat. 'Twill all come back t' me soon.

"Go along wid ye!" exclaimed Dugan. "Would ye be puttin' a goat in th' lake for th' kids t' ride on?"

"Sure!" said Toole enthusiastically. "Sure I would, Dugan. Not th' common goat I wouldn't. But dongola goats I would. Have ye heard of dongola water goats, Casey? Was thim dongola goat skin shoes warranted t' be water-proof?"

Casey wrinkled his brow.

"'Tis like they was, Toole," he said doubtfully. "'Tis like they was warranted t' be, but they wasn't."

"Sure!" cried Toole joyously. "'Tis water-proof th' skin of th' dongola water goats is, like th' skin of th' duck. An' swim? A duck isn't in it wid a water goat. I remimber seein' thim in ould Ireland whin I was a bye, Dugan, swimmin in th' lake of Killarney. Ah, 'twas a purty picture."

"I seem t' remimber thim mesilf," he said. "Not clear, but a bit."

"Sure ye do!" cried Toole. "Many's the time I have rode across th' lake on th' back of a dongola. Me own father, who was a big man in th' ould country, used t' keep a pair of thim for us childer. 'Twas himself fetched thim from Donnegal, Dugan. 'Twas from Donnegal they got th' name of thim, an' 'twas th' name ye give thim that misled me. Donnegoras was what we called thim in th' ould counry—donnegoras from Donnegal. I remimber th' two of thim I had whin I was a kid, Dugan—wan was a Nanny, an' wan was a Billy, an'—"

"Go on home, Mike," said Dugan. "Go on home an' sleep it off!" and the little alderman from the Fourth Ward picked up his hat and coat, and obeyed his orders.

Instituting a new public park and seeing that in every purchase and every contract there is a rake-off for the ring is a big job, and between this and the fight against the rapidly increasing strength of the reform party, Mayor Dugan had his hands more than full. He had no time to think of dongolas, and he did not want to think of them—Toole was the committee on dongolas, and it was his duty to think of them, and to worry about them, if any worry was necessary. But Toole did not worry. He sat down and wrote a letter to his cousin Dennis, official keeper of the zoo in Idlewild Park at Franklin, Iowa.

"Dear Dennis," he wrote. "Have you any dongola goats in your menagery for I want two right away good strong ones answer right away your affectionate cousin alderman Michael Toole."

"Ps monny no object."

When Dennis Toole received this letter he walked through his zoo and considered his animals thoughtfully. The shop-worn brown bear would not do to fill cousin Mike's order; neither would the weather-worn red deer nor the family of variegated tame rabbits. The zoo of Idlewild Park at Franklin was woefully short of dongola goats—in fact, to any but the most imaginative and easily pleased child, it was lacking in nearly every thing that makes a zoo a congress of the world's most rare and thrilling creatures. After all, the nearest thing to a goat was a goat, and goats were plenty in Franklin. Dennis felt an irresistible longing to aid Mike—the longing that comes to any healthy man when a request is accompanied by the legend "Money no object." He wrote that evening to Mike.

"Dear Mike," he wrote. "I've got two good strong dongola goats I can let you have cheap. I'm overstocked with dongolas to-day. I want to get rid of two. Zoo is getting too crowded with all kinds of animals and I don't need so many dongola goats. I will sell you two for fifty dollars. Apiece. What do you want them for? Your affectionate cousin, Dennis Toole, Zoo keeper. PS. Crates extra."

"Casey," said Mike to his friend the saloon keeper when he received this communication, "'tis just as I told ye — dongolas is goats. I have been corrispondin' with wan of th' celibrated animal men regardin' th' dongola water goat, an' I have me eye on two of thim this very minute. But 'twill be ixpinsive, Casey, mighty ixpinsive. Th' dongola water goat is a rare birrd, Casey. They have become extinct in th' lakes of Ireland, an' what few of thim is left in th' worrld is held at outrajeous prices. In th' letter I have from th' animal man, Casey, he wants two hundred dollars apiece for each dongola water goat, an' 'twill be no easy thing for him t' git thim."

"Hasn't he thim in his shop, Mike?" asked Casey.

"He has not, Casey," said the little alderman. "He has no place for thim. Cages he has, an' globes for goldfish, an' birrd cages, but th' size of th' shop l'aves no room for an aquarium, Casey. He has no tank for the preservation of water goats. Hippopotamuses an' alligators an' crocodiles an' dongola water goats an' sea lions he does not keep in stock, Casey, but sinds out an' catches thim whin ordered. He writes that his agints has their eyes on two fine dongolas, an' he has tiligraphed thim t' catch thim."

"Are they near by, Mike?" asked Casey, much interested.

"Naw," said Toole. "'Twill be some time till I git thim. Th' last he heard of thim they were swimmin' in th' Lake of Geneva."

"Is it far, th' lake?" asked Casey.

"I disremimber how far," said Toole. "'Tis in Africa or Asia, or mebby 'tis in Constantinople. Wan of thim countries it is, annyhow."

But to his cousin Dennis he wrote:

"Dear Dennis—I will take them two dongolas. Crate them good and solid. Do not send them till I tell you. Send the bill to me. Your affectionate cousin alderman Michael Toole. Ps Make bill for two hundred dollars a piece. Business is business. This is between us two. M. T."

A Keeper of the Water Goats had been selected with the utmost care, combining in the choice practical politics with a sense of fitness. Timothy Fagan was used to animals—for years he had driven a dumpcart. He was used to children—he had ten or eleven of his own. And he controlled several votes in the Fourth Ward. His elevation from the dump-cart of the street cleaning department to the high office of Keeper of the Water Goats was one that Dugan believed would give general satisfaction.

When the goats arrived in Jeffersonville the two heavy crates were hauled to Alderman Toole's back yard to await the opening of the park, and there Mayor Dugan and Goat Keeper Fagan came to inspect them. Alderman Toole led the way to them with pride, and Mayor Dugan's creased brow almost uncreased as he bent down and peered between the bars of the crates. They were fine goats. Perhaps they looked somewhat more dejected than a goat usually looks—more dirty and down at the heels than a goat often looks— but they were undoubtedly goats. As specimens of ordinary Irish goats they might not have passed muster with a careful buyer, but no doubt they were excellent examples of the dongola.

"Ye have done good, Mike," said the mayor. "Ye have done good! But ain't they mebby a bit off their feed—or something?"

"Off their feed!" said Toole. "An' who wouldn't be, poor things? Mind ye, Dugan, thim is not common goats—thim is dongolas—an' used to bein' in th' wather con-continuous from mornin' till night. 'Tis sufferin' for a swim they be, poor animals. Wance let thim git in th' lake an' ye will see th' difference, Dugan. 'Twill make all th' difference in th' worrld t' thim. 'Tis dyin' for a swim they are."

"Sure!" said the Keeper of the Water Goats. "Ye have done good, Mike," said the mayor again. "Thim dongolas will be a big surprise for th' people."

They were. They surprised the Keeper of the Goats first of all. The day before the park was to be opened to the public the goats were taken to the park and turned over to their official keeper. At eleven o'clock that morning Alderman Toole was leaning against Casey's bar, confidentially pouring into his ear the story of how the dongolas had given their captors a world of trouble, swimming violently to the far reaches of Lake Geneva and hiding among the bulrushes and reeds, when the swinging door of the saloon was banged open and Tim Fagan rushed in. He was mad. He was very mad, but he was a great deal wetter than mad. He looked as if he had been soaked in water over night, and not wrung out in the morning.

"Mike!" he whispered hoarsely, grasping the little alderman by the arm. "I want ye! I want ye down at th' park."

A chill of fear passed over Alderman Toole. He turned his face to Fagan and laid his hand on his shoulder.

"Tim," he demanded, "has annything happened t' th' dongolas?"

"Is annything happened t' th' dongolas!" exclaimed Fagan sarcastically. "Is annything wrong with thim water goats? Oh, no, Toole! Nawthin' has gone wrong with thim! Only they won't go into th' wather, Mike! Is annything gone wrong with thim, did ye say? Nawthin'! They be in good health, but they are not crazy t' be swimmin'. Th' way they do not hanker t' dash into th' water is marvellous, Mike. No water for thim!"

"Hist!" said Toole uneasily, glancing around to see that no one but Casey was in hearing. "Mebby ye have not started thim right, Tim."

"Mebby not," said Fagan angrily. "Mebby I do not know how t' start th' water goat, Toole! Mebby there is one way unbeknownst t' me. If so, I have not tried it. But th' forty-sivin other ways I have tried, an' th' goats will not swim. I have started thim backwards an' I have started thim frontwards, an' I have took thim in by th' horns an' give thim lessons t' swim, an' they will not swim! I have done me duty by thim, Mike, an' I have wrastled with thim, an' rolled in th' lake with thim. Was it t' be swimmin' teacher t' water goats ye got me this job for?"

"Hist!" said Toole again. "Not so loud, Tim! Ye haven't told Dugan have ye?"

"I have not!" said Tim, with anger. "I have not told annybody annything excipt thim goats an' what I told thim is not dacint hearin'. I have conversed with thim in strong language, an' it done no good. No swimmin' for thim! Come on down an' have a chat with thim yersilf, Toole. Come on down an' argue with thim, an persuade thim with th' soft sound of yer voice t' swim. Come on down an' git thim water goats used t' th' water."

"Ye don't understand th' water goat, Tim," said Toole in gentle reproof. "I will show ye how t' handle him," and he went out, followed by the wet Keeper of the Water Goats.

The two water goats stood at the side of the lake, wet and mournful, tied to two strong stakes. They looked weary and meek, for they had had a hard morning, but as soon as they saw Tim Fagan they brightened up. They arose simultaneously on their hind legs and their eyes glittered with deadly hatred. They strained at their ropes, and then, suddenly, panic-stricken, they turned and ran, bringing up at the ends of their ropes with a shock that bent the stout stakes to which they were fastened. They stood still and cowered, trembling.

"Lay hold!" commanded Toole. "Lay hold of a horn of th' brute till I show ye how t' make him swim."

Through the fresh gravel of the beach the four feet of the reluctant goat ploughed deep furrows. It shook its head from side to side, but Toole and Fagan held it fast, and into the water it went.

"Now!" cried Alderman Toole. "Git behind an' push, Tim! Wan! Two! Three! Push!"

Alderman Toole released his hold and Keeper of the Water Goats Fagan pushed. Then they tried the other goat. It was easier to try the other water goat than to waste time hunting up the one they had just tried, for it had gone away. As soon as Alderman Toole let it go, it went. It seemed to want to get to the other end of the park as soon as possible, but it did not take the short cut across the lake—it went around. But it did not mind travel—it went to the farthest part of the park, and it would have gone farther if it could. So Alderman Toole and Keeper Fagan tried the other water goat. That one went straight to the other end of the park. It swerved from a straight line but once, and that was when it shied at a pail of water that was in the way. It did not seem to like water.

In the Franklin Zoo Dennis Toole had just removed the lid of his tin lunch-pail when the telegraph boy handed him the yellow envelope. He turned it over and over, studying its exterior, while the boy went to look at the shop-worn brown bear. The zoo keeper decided that there was no way to find out what was inside of the envelope but to open it. He was ready for the worst. He wondered, unthinkingly, which one of his forty or more cousins was dead, and opened the envelope.

"Dennis Toole, Franklin Zoo," he read, "Dongolas won't swim. How do you make them swim? Telegraph at once. Michael Toole."

He laid the telegram across his knees and looked at it as if it was some strange communication from another sphere. He pushed his hat to one side of his head and scratched the tuft of red hair thus bared.

"'Dongolas won't swim!'" he repeated slowly. "An' how do I make thim swim? I wonder does Cousin Mike take th' goat t' be a fish, or what? I wonder does he take swimmin' to be wan of th' accomplishments of th' goat?" He shook his head in puzzlement, and frowned at the telegram. "Would he be havin' a goat regatta, I wonder, or was he expectin' th' goat t' be a web-footed animal? 'Won't swim!' he repeated angrily. 'Won't swim!' An' what is it to me if they won't swim? Nayther would I swim if I was a goat. 'Tis none of me affair if they will not swim. There was nawthin' said about 'swimmin' goats.' Goats I can give him, an' dongola goats I can give him, an jumpin' goats, an' climbin' goats, an' walkin' goats, but 'tis not in me line t'furnish submarine goats. No, nor goats t' fly up in th' air! Would anny one," he said with exasperation, "would anny one that got a plain order for goats ixpict t' have t' furnish goats that would hop up off th' earth an' make a balloon ascension? 'Tis no fault of Dennis Toole's thim goats won't swim. What will Mike be telegraphin' me nixt, I wonder? 'Dear Dennis: Th' goats won't lay eggs. How do ye make thim?' Bye, have ye a piece of paper t' write an answer t' me cousin Mike on?"

The Keeper of the Water Goats and Alderman Toole were sitting on a rustic bench looking sadly at the water goats when the Jeffersonville telegraph messenger brought them Dennis Toole's answer. Alderman Toole grasped the envelope eagerly and tore it open, and Fagan leaned over his shoulder as he read it:

"Michael Toole, Alderman, Jeffersonville," they read. "Put them in the water and see if they will swim. Dennis Toole."

"Put thim in th' wather!" exclaimed Alderman Toole angrily. "Why don't ye put thim in th' wather, Fagan? Why did ye not think t' put thim in th' wather?" He looked down at his soaking clothes, and his anger increased. "Why have ye been tryin' t' make thim dongolas swim on land, Fagan?" he asked sarcastically. "Or have ye been throwin' thim up in th' air t' see thim swim? Why don't ye put thim in th' wather? Why don't ye follow th' instructions of th' expert dongola water goat man an' put thim in th' wather if ye want thim t' swim?"

Fagan looked at the angry alderman. He looked at the dripping goats.

"So I did, Mike," he said seriously. "We both of us did."

"An' did we!" cried Alderman Toole in mock surprise. "Is it possible we thought t' put thim in th' wather whin we wanted thim t' swim? It was in me mind that we tied thim to a tree an' played ring-around-a-rosy with thim t' induce thim t' swim! Where's a pencil? Where's a piece of paper?" he cried.

He jerked them from the hand of the messenger boy. The afternoon was half worn away. Every minute was precious. He wrote hastily and handed the message to the messenger boy.

"Fagan," he said, as the boy disappeared down the path at a run, "raise up yer spirits an come an' give th' water goats some more instructions in th' ginteel art of swimmin' in th' wather."

Fagan sighed and arose. He walked toward the dejected water goats, and, taking the nearest one by the horns yanked it toward the lake. The goat was too weak to do more than hold back feebly and bleat its disapproval of another bath. The more lessons in swimming it received the less it seemed to like to swim. It had developed a positive hatred of swimming.

Dennis Toole received the second telegram with a savage grin. He had expected it. He opened it with malicious slowness.

"Dennis Toole, Franklin Zoo," he read. "Where do you think I put them to make them swim? They won't swim in the lake. It won't do no good to us for them to swim on dry land. No fooling, now, how do you make them dongolas swim? Answer quick.

"Michael Toole."

He did not have to study out his reply, for he had been considering it ever since he had sent the other telegram. He took a blank from the boy and wrote the answer. The sun was setting when the Jeffersonville messenger delivered it to Alderman Toole.

"Mike Toole, Jeffersonville," it said. "Quit fooling, yourself. Don't you know young dongolas are always water-shy at first? Tie them in the lake and let them soak, and they will learn to swim fast enough. If I didn't know any more about dongolas than you do I would keep clear of them. Dennis Toole."

"Listen to that now," said Alderman Toole, a smile spreading over his face. "An' who ever said I knew annything about water goats, anny how? Th' natural history of th' water goat is not wan of the things usually considered part of th' iducation of th' alderman from th' Fourth Ward, Fagan, but 'tis surprised I am that ye did not know th' goat is like th' soup bean, an' has t' be soaked before usin'. Th' Keeper of th' Water Goat should know th' habits of th' animal, Fagan. Why did ye not put thim in to soak in th' first place? I am surprised at ye!"

"It escaped me mind," said Fagan. "I was thinkin' these was broke t' swimmin' an' did not need t' be soaked. I wonder how long they should be soaked, Mike?"

"'Twill do no harrm t' soak thim over night, anny how," said Toole. "Over night is th' usual soak given t' th' soup-bean an' th' salt mackerel, t' say nawthin' of th' codfish an' others of th' water-goat family. Let th' water goats soak over night, Fagan, an by mornin' they will be ready t' swim like a trout. We will anchor thim in th' lake, Fagan—an' we will say nawthin' t' Dugan. 'Twould be a blow t' Dugan was he t' learn th' dongolas provided fer th' park was young an' wather-shy."

They anchored the water goats firmly in the lake, and left them there to overcome their shyness, which seemed, as Fagan and Toole left them, to be as great as ever. The goats gazed sadly, and bleated longingly, after the two men as they disappeared in the dusk, and when the men had passed entirely out of sight, the goats looked at each other and complained bitterly.

Alderman Toole thoughtfully changed his wet clothes for dry ones before he went to Casey's that evening, for he thought Dugan might be there, and he was. He was there when Toole arrived, and his brow was black. He had had a bad day of it. Everything had gone wrong with him and his affairs. A large lump of his adherents had sloughed off from his party and had affiliated with his opponents, and the evening opposition paper had come out with a red-hot article condemning the administration for reckless extravagance. It had especially condemned Dugan for burdening the city with new bonds to create an unneeded park, and the whole thing had ended with a screech of ironic laughter over the—so the editor called it—fitting capstone of the whole business, the purchase of two dongola goats at perfectly extravagant prices.

"Mike," said the big mayor severely, when the little alderman had offered his greetings, "there is the divil an' all t' pay about thim dongolas. Th' News is full of thim. 'Twill be th' ind of us all if they do not pan out well. Have ye tried thim in th' water yet?"

"Sure!" exclaimed the little alderman with a heartiness he did not feel. "What has me an' Fagan been doin' all day but tryin' thim? Have no fear of th' wather goats, Dugan."

"Do they swim well, Mike?" asked the big mayor kindly, but with a weary heaviness he did not try to conceal.

"Swim!" exclaimed Toole. "Did ye say swim, Dugan? Swim is no name for th' way they rip thro' the wather! 'Twas marvellous t' see thim. Ah, thim dongolas is wonderful animals! Do ye think we could persuade thim t' come out whin we wanted t' come home? Not thim, Dugan! 'Twas all me an' Fagan could do t' pull thim out by main force, an' th' minute we let go of thim, back they wint into th' wather. 'Twas pitiful t' hear th' way they bleated t' be let back into th' wather agin, Dugan, so we let thim stay in for th' night."

"Ye did not let thim loose in th' lake, Mike?" exclaimed the big mayor. "Ye did not let thim be so they could git away?"

"No," said Toole. "No! They'll not git away, Dugan. We anchored thim fast."

"Ye done good, Mike," said the big mayor.

The next morning Keeper of the Water Goats Fagan was down sufficiently early to drag the bodies of the goats out of the lake long before even the first citizen was admitted to the park. Alone, and hastily he hid them in the little tool house, and locked the door on them. Then he went to find Alderman Toole. He found him in the mayor's office, and beckoned him to one side. In hot, quick accents he told him the untimely fate of the dongola water goats, and the mayor—with an eye for everything on that important day—saw the red face of Alderman Toole grow longer and redder; saw the look of pain and horror that overspread it. A chilling fear gripped his own heart.

"Mike," he said. "What's th' matter with th' dongolas?"

It was Fagan who spoke, while the little alderman from the Fourth Ward stood bereft of speech in this awful moment.

"Dugan," he said, "I have not had much ixperience with th' dongola wather goat, an' th' ways an' habits of thim is strange t' me, but if I was t' say what I think, I would say they was over-soaked."

"Over-soaked, Fagan?" said the mayor crossly. "Talk sense, will ye?"

"Sure!" said Fagan. "An' over-soaked is what I say. Thim water goats has all th' looks of bein' soaked too long. I would not say positive, Yer Honour, but that is th' looks of thim. If me own mother was t' ask me I would say th' same, Dugan. 'Soakin' too long done it,' is what I would say."

"You are a fool, Fagan!" exclaimed the big mayor.

"Well," said Fagan mildly, "I have not had much ixperience in soakin' dongolas, if ye mean that, Dugan. I do not set up t' be an expert dongola soaker. I do not know th' rules t' go by. Some may like thim soaked long an' some may like thim soaked not so long, but if I was to say, I would say thim two dongolas at th' park has been soaked a dang sight too long. Th' swim has been soaked clean out of thim."

"Are they sick?" asked the big mayor. "What is th' matter with thim?"

"They do look sick," agreed Fagan, breaking the bad news gently. "I should say they look mighty sick, Dugan. If they looked anny sicker, I would be afther lookin' for a place t' bury thim in. An' I am lookin' for th' place now."

As the truth dawned on the mind of the big mayor, he lost his firm look and sank into a chair. This was the last brick pulled from under his structure of hopes. His head sank upon his breast and for many minutes he was silent, while his aides stood abashed and ill at ease. At last he raised his head and stared at Toole, more in sorrow than in resentfulness.

"Mike," he said, "Mike Toole! What in th' worrld made ye soak thim dongolas?"

"Dugan," pleaded Toole, laying his hand on the big mayor's arm. "Dugan, old man, don't look at me that way. There was nawthin' else t' do but soak thim dongolas. Many's th' time I have seen me old father soakin' th' young dongolas t' limber thim up for swimmin'. 'If iver ye have to do with dongolas, Mike,' he used t' say t' me, 'soak thim well firrst.' So I soaked thim, an' 'tis none of me fault, nor Fagan's either, that they soaked full o' wather. First-class dongolas is wather-proof, as iveryone knows, Dugan, an' how was we t' know thim two was not? How was me an' Fagan t' know their skins would soak in wather like a pillow case? Small blame to us, Dugan."

The big mayor took his head between his hands and stared moodily at the floor.

"Go awn away!" he said after a while. "Ye have done for me an' th' byes, Toole. Ye have soaked us out of office, wan an' all of us. I want t' be alone. It is all over with us. Go awn away."

Toole and the Keeper of the Water Goats stole silently from the room and out into the street. Fagan was the first to speak.

"How was we t' know thim dongolas would soak in wather that way, Toole?" he said defensively. "How was we t' know they was not th' wather-proof kind of dongolas?"

The little alderman from the Fourth Ward walked silently by the Keeper's side. His head was downcast and his hands were clasped beneath the tails of his coat. Suddenly he looked Fagan full in the face.

"'Twas our fault, Fagan," he said. "'Twas all our fault. If we didn't know thim dongolas was wather-proof we should have varnished thim before we put thim in th' lake t' soak. I don't blame you, Fagan, for ye did not know anny better, but I blame mesilf. For I call t' mind now that me father always varnished th' dongolas before he soaked thim overnight. 'Take no chances, Mike,' he used t' say t' me, 'always varnish thim firrst. Some of thim is rubbery an' will not soak up wather, but some is spongy, an' 'tis best t' varnish one an' all of thim.'"

"Think of that now!" exclaimed Fagan with admiration. "Sure, but this natural history is a wonderful science, Toole! To think that thim animals was th' spongyhided dongola water goats of foreign lands, an' used t' bein' varnished before each an' every bath! An' t' me they looked no different from th' goats of me byehood! I was never cut out for a goat keeper, Mike. An' me job on th' dump-cart is gone, too. 'Twill be hard times for Fagan."

"'Twill be hard times for Toole, too," said the little alderman, and they walked on without speaking until Fagan reached his gate.

"Well, anny how," he said with cheerful philosophy, "'tis better t' be us than to be thim dongola water goats—dead or alive. 'Tis not too often I take a bath, Mike, but if I was wan of thim spongy-hided dongolas an' had t' be varnished each time I got in me bath tub, I would stop bathin' for good an' all."

He looked toward the house.

"I'll not worry," he said. "Maggie will be sad t' hear th' job is gone, but she would have took it harder t' know her Tim was wastin' his time varnishin' th' slab side of a spongy goat."

II. MR. BILLINGS'S POCKETS

On the sixteenth of June Mr. Rollin Billings entered his home at Westcote very much later than usual, and stealing upstairs, like a thief in the night, he undressed and dropped into bed. In two minutes he was asleep, and it was no wonder, for by that time it was five minutes after three in the morning, and Mr. Billings's usual bedtime was ten o'clock. Even when he was delayed at his office he made it an invariable rule to catch the nine o'clock train home.

When Mrs. Billings awoke the next—or, rather, that same—morning, she gazed a minute at the thin, innocent face of her husband, and was in the satisfied frame of mind that takes an unexpected train delay as a legitimate excuse, when she happened to cast her eyes upon Mr. Billings's coat, which was thrown carelessly over the foot of the bed. Protruding from one of the side pockets was a patent nursing-bottle, half full of milk. Instantly Mrs. Billings was out of bed and searching Mr. Billings's other pockets. To her horror her search was fruitful.

In a vest pocket she found three false curls, or puffs of hair, such as ladies are wearing to-day to increase the abundance of their own, and these curls were of a rich brownish red. Finally, when she dived into his trousers pocket, she found twelve acorns carefully wrapped in a lady's handkerchief, with the initials "T. M. C." embroidered in one corner.

All these Mrs. Billings hid carefully in her upper bureau drawer and proceeded to dress. When at length she awakened Mr. Billings, he yawned, stretched, and then, realizing that getting-up time had arrived, hopped briskly out of bed.

"You got in late last night," said Mrs. Billings pleasantly.

If she had expected Mr. Billings to cringe and cower she was mistaken. He continued to dress, quite in his usual manner, as if he had a clear conscience.

"Indeed I did, Mary," he said. "It was three when I entered the house, for the clock was just striking."

"Something must have delayed you," suggested Mrs. Billings.

"Otherwise, dear," said Mr. Billings, "I should have been home much sooner.

"Probably," said Mrs. Billings, suddenly assuming her most sarcastic tone, as she reached into her bureau drawer and drew out the patent nursing-bottle, "this had something to do with your being delayed!"

Mr. Billings looked at the nursing-bottle, and then he drew out his watch and looked at that.

"My dear," he said, "you are right. It did. But I now have just time to gulp down my coffee and catch my train. To-night, when I return from town, I will tell you the most remarkable story of that nursing-bottle, and how it happened to be in my pocket, and in the mean time I beg you — I most sincerely beg you — to feel no uneasiness."

With this he hurried out of the room, and a few moments later his wife saw him running for his train.

All day Mrs. Billings was prey to the most disturbing thoughts, and as soon as dinner was finished that evening she led the way into the library.

"Now, Rollin?" she said, and without hesitation Mr. Billings began.

I. THE PATENT NURSING-BOTTLE

You have (he said), I know, met Lemuel, the coloured elevator boy in our office building, and you know what a pleasant, accommodating lad he is. He is the sort of boy for whom one would gladly do a favour, for he is always so willing to do favours for others, but I was thinking nothing of this when I stepped from my office at exactly five o'clock yesterday evening. I was thinking of nothing but getting home to dinner as soon as possible, and was just stepping into the elevator when Lemuel laid his hand gently on my arm.

"I beg yo' pahdon, Mistah Billings," he said politely, "but would yo' do me a favour?"

"Certainly, Lemuel," I said; "how much can I lend you?"

"'Tain't that, sah," he said. "I wish t' have a word or two in private with yo'. Would yo' mind steppin' back into yo' office until I git these folks out of th' buildin', so's I can speak to yo'?"

I knew I had still half an hour before my six-two train, and I was not unwilling to do Lemuel a favour, so I went back to my office as he desired, and waited there until he appeared, which was not until he had taken all the tenants down in his elevator. Then he opened the door and came in. With him was the young man I had often seen in the office next to mine, as I passed, and a young woman on whom I had never set my eyes before. No sooner had they opened the door than the young man began to speak, and Lemuel stood unobtrusively to one side.

"Mr. Billings," said the young man, "you may think it strange that I should come to you in this way when you and I are hardly acquaintances, but I have often observed you passing my door, and have noted your kind-looking face, and the moment I found this trouble upon me I instantly thought of you as the one man who would be likely to help me out of my difficulty."

While he said this I had time to study his face, and also to glance at the young woman, and I saw that he must, indeed, be in great trouble. I also saw that the young woman was pretty and modest and that she, also, was in great distress. I at once agreed to help him, provided I should not be made to miss the six-thirty train, for I saw I was already too late for the six-two.

"Good!" he cried. "For several years Madge — who is this young lady — and I have been in love, and we wish to be married this evening, but her father and my father are waiting at the foot of the elevator at this minute, and they have been waiting there all day. There is no other way for us to leave the building, for the foot of the stairs is also the foot of the elevator, and, in fact, when I last peeped, Madge's father was sitting on the bottom step. It is now exactly fifteen minutes of six, and at six o'clock they mean to come up and tear Madge and me away, and have us married."

"To — " I began.

"To each other," said the young man with emotion.

"But I thought that was what you wanted?" I exclaimed.

"Not at all! Not at all!" said the young man, and the young woman added her voice in protest, too. "I am the head of the Statistical Department of the Society for the Obtaining of a Uniform National Divorce Law, and the work in that department has convinced me beyond a doubt that forced marriages always end unhappily. In eighty-seven thousand six hundred and four cases of forced marriages that I have tabulated I have found that eighty-seven thousand six hundred and three have been unhappy. In the face of such statistics Madge and I dare not allow ourselves to be married against our wills. We insist on marrying voluntarily."

"That could be easily arranged," I ventured to say, "in view of the fact that both your fathers wish you to be married."

"Not at all," said Madge, with more independence than I had thought her capable of; "because my father and Henry's father are gentlemen of the old school. I would not say anything against either father, for in ordinary affairs I they are two most suave and charming old gentlemen, but in this they hold to the old-school idea that children should allow their parents to select their life-partners, and they insist that Henry and I allow ourselves to be forced to marry each other. And that, in spite of the statistics Henry has shown them. Our whole happiness depends on our getting out of this building before they can come up and get us. That is why we appeal to you."

"If you still hesitate, after what Madge has said," said Henry, pulling a large roll of paper out of his pocket, "here are the statistics."

"Very well," I said, "I will help you, if I can do so and not miss the six-thirty train. What is your plan?"

"It is very simple," said Henry. "Our fathers are both quite near-sighted, and as six o'clock draws near they will naturally become greatly excited and nervous, and, therefore, less observant of small things. I have brought with me some burnt cork with which I will blacken my face, and I will change clothes with Lemuel, and, in the one moment necessary to escape, my father will not recognize me. Lemuel, on the other hand, will whiten his face with some powder that Madge has brought, and will wear my clothes, and in the excitement my father will seize him instead of me."

"Excellent," I said, "but what part do I play in this?"

"This part," said Henry, "you will wear, over your street clothes, a gown that Madge has brought in her suit-case and a hat that she has also brought, both of which her father will easily recognize, while Madge will redden her face with rouge, muss her hair, don a torn, calico dress, and with a scrub-rag and a mop in her hands easily pass for a scrub-woman.

"And then?" I asked.

"Then you and Lemuel will steal cautiously down the stairs, as if you were Madge and I seeking to escape, while Madge and I, as Lemuel and the scrub-woman, will go down by the elevator. My father and Madge's father will seize you and Lemuel—"

"And I shall appear like a fool when they discover I am a respectable business man rigged up in woman's clothes," I said.

"Not at all," said Madge, "for Henry and I have thought of that. You must play your part until you see that henry and I have escaped from the elevator and have left the building, and that is all. I have had the forethought to prepare an alibi for you. As soon as you see that Henry and I are safe outside the building, you must become very indignant, and insist that you are a respectable married woman, and in proof you must hand my father the contents of this package. He will be convinced immediately and let you go, and then Lemuel can run you up to your office and you can take off my dress and hat and catch the six-thirty train without trouble." She then handed me a small parcel, which I slipped into my coat pocket.

When this had been agreed upon she and Henry left the office and I took the hat and dress from the suit-case and put them on, while Lemuel put on Henry's suit and whitened his face. This took but a few minutes, and we went into the hall and found Henry and Madge already waiting for us. Henry was blackened into a good likeness of Lemuel, and Madge was quite a mussy scrub-woman. They immediately entered the elevator and began to descend slowly, while Lemuel and I crept down the stairs.

Lemuel and I kept as nearly as possible opposite the elevator, so that we might arrive at the foot of the stairs but a moment before Madge and Henry, and we could hear the two fathers shuffling on the street floor, when suddenly, as we reached the third floor, we heard a whisper from Henry in the elevator. The elevator had stuck fast between the third and fourth floors. As with one mind, Lemuel and I seated ourselves on a step and waited until Henry should get the elevator running again and could proceed to the street floor.

For a while we could hear no noise but the grating of metal on metal as Henry worked with the starting lever of the elevator, and then we heard the two voices of the fathers.

"It is a ruse," said one father. "They are pretending the elevator is stuck, and when we grow impatient and start up the stairs they will come down with a rush and escape us."

"But we are not so silly as that," said the other father. "We will stay right here and wait until they come down."

At that Lemuel and I settled ourselves more comfortably, for there was nothing else to do. I cursed inwardly as I felt the minutes slip by and knew that half-past six had come and gone, but I was sure you would not like to have me desert those two poor lovers who were fighting to ward off the statistics, so I sat still and silent. So did Lemuel.

I do not know how long I sat there, for it was already dark in the narrow stairway, but it must have been a long time. I drowsed off, and I was finally awakened by Lemuel tugging at my sleeve, and I knew that Henry had managed to start the elevator again. Lemuel and I hastened our steps, and just as the elevator was coming into sight below the second floor we were seen by the two fathers. For an instant they hesitated, and then they seized us. At the same time the elevator door opened and Henry and Madge came out, and the two fathers hardly glanced at them as they went out of the door into the street.

As soon as I saw that they were safe I feigned great indignation, and so did Lemuel.

"Unhand me, sir!" I cried. "Who do you think I am? I am a re-spectable married lady, leaving the building with her husband. Unhand me!"

Instead of doing so, however, the father that had me by the arm drew me nearer to the hall light. As he did so he stared closely at my face.

"Morgan," he said to the other father, "this is not my daughter. My daughter did not have a moustache."

"Indeed, I am not your daughter," I said; "I am a respectable married lady, and here is the proof."

With that I reached for the package Madge had given me, but it was in my coat-pocket, underneath the dress I had on, and it was only with great difficulty and by raising one side of the skirt that I was able to get it. I unwrapped it and showed it to the father that had me by the arm. It was the patent nursing-bottle.

When Mr. Billings had finished his relation his wife sat for a moment in silence. Then she said:

"And he let you go?"

"Yes, of course," said Mr. Billings; "he could not hold me after such proof as that, and Lemuel ran me up to my office, where I changed my hat and took off the dress. I knew it was late, and I did not know what train I could catch, but I made haste, and, on the way down in the elevator, I felt in my pocket to see if I had my commutation ticket, when my hand struck the patent nursing-bottle. My first impulse was to drop it in the car, but on second thought I decided to keep it, for I knew that when you saw it and heard the story you would understand perfectly why I was detained last night."

"Yes?" said Mrs. Billings questioningly. "But, my dear, all that does not account for these."

As she said that she drew from her workbasket the three auburn-red curls.

"Oh, those!" said Mr. Billings, after a momentary hesitation. "I was about to tell you about those."

"Do so!" said Mrs. Billings coldly. "I am listening."

II. THE THREE AUBURN-RED CURLS

When I went down in the elevator (said Mr. Billings) with the nursing-bottle in my pocket, I had no thought but to get to the train as soon as possible, for I saw by the clock in my office that I had just time to catch the eleven-nine if I should not be delayed. Therefore, as soon as I was outside the building I started to run, but when I reached the corner and was just about to step on a passing street-car a hand was laid on my arm, and I turned to see who was seeking to detain me. It was a woman in the most pitiable rags, and on her arm she carried a baby so thin and pale that I could scarcely believe it lived.

One glance at the child showed me that it was on the verge of death by starvation, and this was confirmed by the moans of the mother, who begged me for humanity's sake to give her money with which to provide food for the child, even though I let her, herself, starve. You know, my dear, you never allow me to give money to street beggars, and I remembered this, but at the same time I remembered the patent nursing-bottle I still carried in my pocket.

Without hesitation I drew the patent nursing-bottle from my pocket and told the mother to allow the infant to have a sufficient quantity of milk it contained to sustain the child's life until she could procure other alms or other aid. With a cry of joy the mother took the nursing-bottle and pressed it to the poor baby's lips, and it was with great pleasure I saw the rosy colour return to the child's cheeks. The sadness of despair that had shadowed the mother's face also fled, and I could see that already she was looking on life with a more optimistic view.

I verily believe the child could have absorbed the entire contents of the bottle, but I had impressed upon the mother that she was to give the child only sufficient to sustain life, not to suffice it until it was grown to manhood or womanhood, and when the bottle was half-emptied the mother returned it to me. How much time all this occupied I do not know, but the child took the milk with extreme slowness. I may say that it took the milk drop by drop. A great deal of time must have elapsed.

But when the mother had returned the patent nursing-bottle to me and saw how impatient I was to be gone, she still retained her hold upon my arm.

"Sir," she said, "you have undoubtedly saved the life of my child, and I only regret that I cannot repay you for all it means to me. But I cannot. Stay!" she cried, when I was about to pull my arm away. "Has your wife auburn-red hair?"

"No," I said, "she has not, her hair is a most beautiful black."

"No matter," said the poor woman, putting her hand to her head. "Some day she may wish to change the colour of her hair to auburn-red, which is easily done with a little bleach and a little dye, and should she do so these may come handy;" and with that she slipped something soft and fluffy into my hand and fled into the night. When I looked, I saw in my hand the very curls you hold there. My first impulse was to drop them in the street, but I remembered that the poor woman had not given them to me, but to you, and that it was my duty to bring them home to you, so I slipped them into my pocket.

When Mr. Billings had ended this recital of what had happened to him his wife said:

"Huh!"

At the same time she tossed the curls into the grate, where they shrivelled up, burst into blue smoke, and shortly disappeared in ashes.

"That is a very likely story," she said, "but it does not explain how this came to be in your pocket."

Saying this she drew from her basket the handkerchief and handed it to Mr. Billings.

"Hah!" he exclaimed. For a moment he turned the rolled-up handkerchief over and over, and then he cautiously opened it. At the sight of the twelve acorns he seemed somewhat surprised, and when the initials "T. M. C." on the corner of the handkerchief caught his eye he blushed.

"You are blushing—you are disturbed," said Mrs. Billings severely.

"I am," said Mr. Billings, suddenly recovering himself; "and no wonder."

"And no wonder, indeed!" said Mrs Billings. "Perhaps, then, you can tell me how those acorns and that handkerchief came to be in your pocket."

"I can," said Mr. Billings, "and I will."

"You had better," said Mrs. Billings.

III. THE TWELVE ACORNS AND THE LADY'S HANDKERCHIEF

You may have noticed, my dear (said Mr. Billings), that the initials on that handkerchief are "T. M. C.," and I wish you to keep that in mind, for it has a great deal to do with this story. Had they been anything else that handkerchief would not have found its way into my pocket; and when you see how those acorns and that handkerchief, and the half-filled nursing-bottle and the auburn-red curls all combined to keep me out of my home until the unearthly hour of three A. M., you will forget the unjust suspicions which I too sadly fear you now hold against me, and you will admit that a half-filled patent nursing-bottle, a trio of curls, a lady's handkerchief and twelve acorns were the most natural things in the world to find in my pockets.

When I had left the poor woman with her no-longer-starving baby I hurriedly glanced into a store window, and by the clock there saw it was twenty minutes of one and that I had exactly time to catch the one o'clock train, which is the last train that runs to Westcote. I glanced up and down the street, but not a car was in sight, and I knew I could not afford to wait long if I wished to catch that train. There was but one thing to do, and that was to take a cab, and, as luck would have it, at that moment an automobile cab came rapidly around the corner. I raised my voice and my arm, and the driver saw or heard me, for he made a quick turn in the street and drew up at the curb beside me. I hastily gave him the directions, jumped in and slammed the door shut, and the auto-cab immediately started forward at what seemed to me unsafe speed.

We had not gone far when something in the fore part of the automobile began to thump in a most alarming manner, and the driver slackened his speed, drew up to the curb and stopped. He opened the door and put his head in.

"Something's gone wrong," he said, "but don't you worry. I'll have it fixed in no time, and then I can put on more speed and I'll get you there in just the same time as if nothing had happened."

When he said this I was perfectly satisfied, for he was a nice-looking man, and I lay back, for I was quite tired out, it was so long past my usual bedtime; and the driver went to work, doing things I could not understand to the fore part of the automobile, where the machinery is. I remember thinking that the cushions of this auto-mobile were unusually soft, and then I must have dozed off, and when I opened my eyes I did not know how much time had elapsed, but the driver was still at work and I could hear him swear-ing. He seemed to be having a great deal of trouble, so I got out of the automobile, intending to tell him that perhaps I had better try to get a car, after all. But his actions when he saw me were most unex-pected. He waved the wrench he held in his hand, and ordered me to get back into the automobile, and I did. I supposed he was afraid he would lose his fare and tip, but in a few minutes he opened the door again and spoke to me.

"Now, sport," he said, "there ain't no use thinkin' about gettin' that train, because it's gone, and I may as well say now that you've got to come with me, unless you want me to smash your head in. The fact is, this ain't no public automobile, and I hadn't no right to take you for a passenger. This automobile belongs to a lady and I'm her hired chauffeur, and she's at a bridge-whist party in a house on Fifth Avenue, and I'm supposed to be waiting outside that house. One-fifteen o'clock was the time she said she would be out. But I thought maybe I might make a dollar or two for myself instead of waiting there all that time, and she would never know it. And now it is nearly two o'clock, and if I go back alone she will be raving mad, and I'll get my discharge and no references, and my poor wife and six children will have to starve. So you will have to go with me and explain how it was that I wasn't there at one-fifteen o'clock."

"My friend," I said, "I am sorry for you, but I do not see how it would help you, should I refuse to go and you should, as you say, smash my head in."

"Don't you worry none about that," he said. "If I smashed your head in, as I could do easy enough with this wrench, I'd take what was left of you up some dark street, and lay you on the pavement and run the machine across you once or twice, and then take you to a hospital, and that would be excuse enough. You'd be another 'Killed by an Automobile,' and I'd be the hero that picked you up and took you to the hospital."

"Well," I said, "under the circumstances I shall go with you, not because you threaten me, but because your poor wife and six children are threatened with starvation."

"Good!" he said. "And now all you have to do is to think of what the excuse you will give my lady boss will be."

With that he lay back against the cushions and waited. He seemed to feel that the matter did not concern him any more, and that the rest of it lay with me.

"Go ahead!" I said to him. "I have no idea what I shall tell your mistress, but since I have lost the last train I must try to catch the two o'clock trolley car to Westeote, and I do not wish to spend any more time than necessary on this business. Make all the haste possible, and as we go I shall think what I will say when we get there."

The driver got out and took his seat and started the car. I was worried, indeed, my dear. I tried to think of something plausible to tell the young man's employer; something that would have an air of self-proof, when suddenly I remembered the half-filled nursing-bottle and the three auburn-red curls. Why should I not tell the lady that a poor mother, while proceeding down Fifth Avenue from her scrub-woman job, had been taken suddenly ill, and that I, being near, had insisted that this automobile help me convey the woman to her home, which we found, alas! to be in the farthest districts of Brooklyn? Then I would produce the three auburn-red curls and the half-filled nursing-bottle as having been left in the automobile by the woman, and this proof would suffice.

I had fully decided on this when the automobile stopped in front of a large house in Fifth Avenue, and I had time to tell the driver that I had thought of the proper thing to say, but that was all, for the waiting lady came down the steps in great anger, and was about to begin a good scolding, when she noticed me sitting in her automobile.

If she had been angry before she was now furious, and she was
the kind of young woman who can be extremely furious when she
tries. I think nothing in the world could have calmed her had she
not caught sight of my face by the light of two strong lamps on a
passing automobile. She saw in my face what you see there now,
my dear—the benevolent, fatherly face of a settled-down, trustwor-
thy, married man of past middle age—and as if by magic her anger
fled and she burst into tears.

"Oh, sir!" she cried, "I do not know who you are, nor how you
happen to be in my car, but at this moment I am homeless and
friendless. I am alone in the world, and I need advice. Let me get
into the car beside you—"

"Miss," I said, "I do not like to disoblige you, but I can never allow
myself to be in an automobile at this time of night with a strange
woman, unchaperoned."

These words seemed almost more than she could bear, and my
heart was full of pity, but, just as I was about to spring from the
automobile and rush away, I saw on the walk the poor woman to
whose baby I had given the half of the contents of the patent nursing-bottle. I called her and made her get into the automobile, and
then I let the young woman enter.

"Now," I said, "where to?"

"That," she said, "is what I do not know. When I left my home this
evening I left it forever, and I left a note of farewell to my father,
which he must have received and read by this time, and if I went
back he would turn me from the door in anger, for he is a gentle-
man of the old school."

When I heard these words I was startled. "Can it be," I asked,
"that you have a brother henry?"

"I have," she admitted; "Henry Corwin is his name." This was the
name of the young man I had helped that very evening to marry
Madge. I told her to proceed.

"My father," she said, "has been insisting that I marry a man I do
not love, and things have come to such a point that I must either
accede or take things into my own hands. I agreed to elope this

evening with the man I love, for he had long wished me to elope with him. I was to meet him outside his house at exactly one-fifteen o'clock, and I told him that if I was not there promptly he might know I had changed my mind. When the time came for me to hasten to him in my automobile, which was then to hurry us to a waiting minister, my automobile was not here. Unfortunately I did not know my lover's address, for I had left it in the card pocket in this automobile. I knew not what to do. As the time passed and my automobile did not appear I knew that my lover had decided that I was not coming, and had gone away into his house. Now I cannot go home, for I have no home. I cannot so lower my pride as to ring the bell of his house and say I wish to be forgiven and married even yet. What shall I do?"

For answer I felt in the card pocket of the automobile and drew out the address of her lover, and without hesitation I gave the address to the chauffeur. In a few minutes we were there. Leaving the young woman in the car with the poor woman, I got out and surveyed the house. It was unpromising. Evidently all the family but the young man were away for the summer, and the doors and windows were all boarded up. There was not a bell to ring. I pounded on the boards that covered the door, but it was unavailing. The young woman called to me that the young man lived in the front room of the topmost floor, and could not hear me, and I glanced up and saw that one window alone of all those in the house was not boarded up. Instantly I hopped upon the seat beside the driver and said, "Central Park."

We dashed up Fifth Avenue and into the Park at full speed, and when we were what I considered far enough in I ordered him to stop, and hurrying up a low bank I began to grope among the leaves of last year under the trees. I was right. In a few minutes I had filled my pockets with acorns, was back in the car, and we were hurrying toward the house of the lover, when I saw standing on a corner a figure I instantly recognized as Lemuel, the elevator boy, and at the same time I remembered that Lemuel spent his holidays pitching for a ball nine, He was just the man I needed, and I stopped and made him get into the car. In a minute more we were before the house again, and I handed Lemuel a fistful of acorns. He drew back and threw them with all his strength toward the upper window.

My dear, will you believe it? Those acorns were wormy! They were light. They would not carry to the window, but scattered like bits of chips when they had travelled but half-way. I was upset, but Lemuel was not. He ordered the chauffeur to drive to lower Sixth Avenue with all speed, in order that he might get a baseball. With this he said he could hit any mark, and we had started in that direction when, passing a restaurant on Broadway, I saw emerge Henry and Madge.

"Better far," I said to myself, "put this young woman in charge of her brother and his new wife than leave her to elope alone," and I made the chauffeur draw up beside them. Hastily I explained the situation, and where we were going at that moment, and Henry and Madge laughed in unison.

"Madge," said Henry, "we had no trouble making wormy acorns travel through the air, had we?" And both laughed again. At this I made them get into the automobile, and while we returned to the lover's house I made them explain. It was very simple, and I had just tied a dozen acorns tightly in my handkerchief, making a ball to throw at the window, when the poor woman with the baby noticed that the window was partly open. I asked Lemuel if he could throw straight enough to throw the handkerchief-ball into the window, and he said he could, and took the handkerchief, but a brighter idea came to me, and I turned to the eloping young lady.

"Let me have your handkerchief, if it has your initials on it," I said; "for when he sees that fall into his room he will know you are here. He will not think you are forward, coming to him alone, for he will know you could never have thrown the handkerchief, even if loaded with acorns, to such a height. It will be your message to him."

At this, which I do pride myself was a suggestion worthy of myself, all were delighted, and while I modestly tied twelve acorns in the handkerchief on which were the initials "T. M. C.," all the others cheered. Even the woman from whom I had received the three auburn-red curls cheered, and the baby that was half-filled out of the patent nursing-bottle crowed with joy. But the chauffeur honked his honker. Lemuel took the handkerchief full of acorns in his hand and drew back his famous left arm, when suddenly Theodora Mitchell

Corwin—for that was the eloping young lady's name—shrieked, and looking up we saw her lover at the window. He gave an answering yell and disappeared, and Lemuel let his left arm fall and handed me the handkerchief-ball.

In the excitement I dropped it into my pocket, and it was not until I was on the car for Westcote that I discovered it, and then, not wishing to be any later in getting home, I did not go back to give it to Theodora Mitchell Corwin; in fact, I did not know where she had eloped to. Nor could I give it to Madge or Henry, for they had gone on their wedding journey as soon as they saw Theodora and her lover safely eloped.

I had no right to give it to the poor woman with the baby, even if she had not immediately disappeared into her world of poverty, and it certainly did not belong to Lemuel, nor could I have given it to him, for he took the ten dollars the lover gave him and stayed out so late that he was late to work this morning and was discharged. He said he was going back to Texas. So I brought the handkerchief and the twelve acorns home, knowing you would be interested in hearing their story.

When Mr. Billings had thus finished his relation of the happenings of his long evening, Mrs. Billings was thoughtful for a minute. Then she said:

"But Rollin, when I spoke to you of the handkerchief and the twelve acorns you blushed, and said you had reason to blush. I see nothing in this kind action you did to cause a blush."

"I blushed," said Mr. Billings, "to think of the lie I was going to tell Theodora Merrill Corwin—"

"I thought you said her name was Theodora Mitchell Corwin," said Mrs. Billings.

"Mitchell or Merill," said Mr. Billings. "I cannot remember exactly which."

For several minutes Mrs. Billings was silent. Occasionally she would open her mouth as if to ask a question, but each time she closed it again without speaking. Mr. Billings sat regarding his wife with what, in a man of less clear conscience, might be called anxiety.

At length Mrs. Billings put her sewing into her sewing-basket and arose.

"Rollin," she said, "I have enjoyed hearing you tell your experiences greatly. I can say but one thing: Never in your life have you deceived me. And you have not deceived me now."

For half an hour after this Mr. Billings sat alone, thinking.

III. OUR FIRST BURGLAR

When our new suburban house was completed I took Sarah out to see it, and she liked it all but the stairs.

"Edgar," she said, when she had ascended to the second floor, "I don't know whether it is imagination or not, but it seems to me that these stairs are funny, some way. I can't understand it. They are not a long flight, and they are not unusually steep, but they seem to be unusually wearying. I never knew a short flight to tire me so, and I have climbed many flights in the six years we have lived in flats."

"Perhaps, Sarah," I said, with mild dissimulation, "you are unusually tired to-day."

The fact was that I had planned those stairs myself, and for a particular reason I had made the rise of each step three inches more than the customary height, and in this way I had saved two steps. I had also made the tread of the steps unusually narrow; and the reason was that I had found, from long experience, that stair carpet wears first on the tread of the steps, where the foot falls. By making the steps tall enough to save two, and by making the tread narrow, I reduced the wear on the carpet to a minimum. I believe in economy where it is possible. For the same reason I had the stair banisters made wide, with a saddle-like top to the newel post, to tempt my son and daughter to slide downstairs. The less they used the stairs the longer the carpet would last.

I need hardly say that Sarah has a fear of burglars; most women have. As for myself, I prefer not to meet a burglar. It is all very well to get up in the night and prowl about with a pistol in one hand, seeking to eliminate the life of a burglar, and some men may like it; but I am of a very excitable nature, and I am sure that if I did find a burglar and succeeded in shooting him, I should be in such an excited state that I could not sleep again that night — and no man can afford to lose his night's rest.

There are other objections to shooting a burglar in the house, and these objections apply with double force when the house and its furnishings are entirely new. Although some of the rugs in our house were red, not all of them were; and I had no guarantee that if

I shot a burglar he would lie down on a red rug to bleed to death. A burglar does not consider one's feelings, and would be quite as apt to bleed on a green rug, and spoil it, as not. Until burglarizing is properly regulated and burglars are educated, as they should be, in technical burglary schools, we cannot hope that a shot burglar will staunch his wound until he can find a red rug to lie down on.

And there are still other objections to shooting a burglar. If all burglars were fat, one of these would be removed; but perhaps a thin burglar might get in front of my revolver, and in that case the bullet would be likely to go right through him and continue on its way, and perhaps break a mirror or a cut-glass dish. I am a thin man myself, and if a burglar shot at me he might damage things in the same way.

I thought all these things over when we decided to build in the suburbs, for Sarah is very nervous about burglars, and makes me get up at the slightest noise and go poking about. Only the fact that no burglar had ever entered our flat at night had prevented what might have been a serious accident to a burglar, for I made it a rule, when Sarah wakened me on such occasions, to waste no time, but to go through the rooms as hastily as possible and get back to bed; and at the speed I travelled I might have bumped into a burglar in the dark and knocked him over, and his head might have struck some hard object, causing concussion of the brain; and as a burglar has a small brain a small amount of concussion might have ruined it entirely. But as I am a slight man it might have been my brain that got concussed. A father of a family has to think of these things.

The nervousness of Sarah regarding burglars had led me in this way to study the subject carefully, and my adoption of jet-black pajamas as nightwear was not due to cowardice on my part. I properly reasoned that if a burglar tried to shoot me while I was rushing around the house after him in the darkness, a suit of black pajamas would somewhat spoil his aim, and, not being able to see me, he would not shoot at all. In this way I should save Sarah the nerve shock that would follow the explosion of a pistol in the house. For Sarah was very much more afraid of pistols than of burglars. I am sure there were only two reasons why I had never killed a burglar with a pistol: one was that no burglar had ever entered our flat, and the other was that I never had a pistol.

But I knew that one is much less protected in a suburb than in town, and when I decided to build I studied the burglar protection matter most carefully. I said nothing to Sarah about it, for fear it would upset her nerves, but for months I considered every method that seemed to have any merit, and that would avoid getting a burglar's blood—or mine—spattered around on our new furnishings. I desired some method by which I could finish up a burglar properly without having to leave my bed, for although Sarah is brave enough in sending me out of bed to catch a burglar, I knew she must suffer severe nerve strain during the time I was wandering about in the dark. Her objection to explosives had also to be considered, and I really had to exercise my brain more than common before I hit upon what I may now consider the only perfect method of handling burglars.

Several things coincided to suggest my method. One of these was Sarah's foolish notion that our silver must, every night, be brought from the dining-room and deposited under our bed. This I considered a most foolhardy tempting of fate. It coaxed any burglar who ordinarily would have quietly taken the silver from the dining-room and have then gone away peacefully, to enter our room. The knowledge that I lay in bed ready at any time to spring out upon him would make him prepare his revolver, and his nervousness might make him shoot me, which would quite upset Sarah's nerves. I told Sarah so, but she had a hereditary instinct for bringing the silver to the bedroom, and insisted. I saw that in the suburban house this, would be continued as "bringing the silver upstairs," and a trial of my carpet-saving stairs suggested to me my burglar-defeating plan. I had the apparatus built into the house, and I had the house planned to agree with the apparatus.

For several months after we moved into the house I had no burglars, but I felt no fear of them in any event. I was prepared for them.

In order not to make Sarah nervous, I explained to her that my invention of a silver-elevator was merely a time-saving device. From the top of the dining-room sideboard I ran upright tracks through the ceiling to the back of the hall above, and in these I placed a glass case, which could be run up and down the tracks like a dumbwaiter. All our servant had to do when she had washed the silver was to put it in the glass case, and I had attached to the top of the case a stout steel cable which ran to the ceiling of the hall above, over a pulley, and so to our bedroom, which was at the front of the hall upstairs. By this means I could, when I was in bed, pull the cable, and the glass case of silver would rise to the second floor. Our bedroom door opened upon the hall, and from the bed I could see the glass case; but in order that I might be sure that the silver was there I put a small electric light in the case and kept it burning all night. Sarah was delighted with this arrangement, for in the morning all I had to do was to pay out the steel cable and the silver would descend to the dining-room, and the maid could have the table all set by the time breakfast was ready. Not once did Sarah have a suspicion that all this was not merely a household economy, but my burglar trap.

On the sixth of August, at two o'clock in the morning, Sarah awakened me, and I immediately sat straight up in bed. There was an undoubtable noise of sawing, and I knew at once that a burglar was entering our home. Sarah was trembling, and I knew she was getting nervous, but I ordered her to remain calm.

"Sarah," I said, in a whisper, "be calm! There is not the least danger. I have been expecting this for some time, and I only hope the burglar has no dependent family or poor old mother to support. Whatever happens, be calm and keep perfectly quiet."

With that I released the steel cable from the head of my bed and let the glass case full of silver slide noiselessly to the sideboard.

"Edgar!" whispered Sarah in agonized tones, "are you giving him our silver?"

"Sarah!" I whispered sternly, "remember what I have just said. Be calm and keep perfectly quiet." And I would say no more.

In a very short time I heard the window below us open softly, and I knew the burglar was entering the parlour from the side porch. I counted twenty, which I had figured would be the time required for him to reach the dining-room, and then, when I was sure he must have seen the silver shining in the glass case, I slowly pulled on the steel cable and raised case and silver to the hall above. Sarah began to whisper to me, but I silenced her.

What I had expected happened. The burglar, seeing the silver rise through the ceiling, left the dining-room and went into the hall. There, from the foot of the stairs, he could see the case glowing in the hall above, and without hesitation he mounted the stairs. As he reached the top I had a good view of him, for he was silhouetted against the light that glowed from the silver case. He was a most brutal looking fellow of the prize-fighting type, but I almost laughed aloud when I saw his build. He was short and chunky. As he stepped forward to grasp the silver case, I let the steel cable run through my fingers, and the case and its precious contents slid noiselessly down to the dining-room. For only one instant the burglar seemed disconcerted, then he turned and ran downstairs again.

This time I did not wait so long to draw up the silver. I hardly gave him time to reach the dining-room door before I jerked the cable, and the case was glowing in the upper hall. The burglar immediately stopped, turned, and mounted the stairs, but just as he reached the top I let the silver slide down again, and he had to turn and descend. Hardly had he reached the bottom step before I had the silver once more in the upper hall.

The burglar was a gritty fellow and was not to be so easily defeated. With some word which I could not catch, but which I have no doubt was profane, or at least vulgar, he dashed up the stairs, and just as his hand touched the case I let the silver drop to the dining-room. I smiled as I saw his next move. He carefully removed his coat and vest, rolled up his sleeves, and took off his collar. This evidently meant that he intended to get the silver if it took the whole night, and nothing could have pleased me more. I lay in my comfortable bed fairly shaking with suppressed laughter, and had to stuff a corner of a pillow in my mouth to smother the sound of my mirth. I did not allow the least pity for the unfortunate fellow to weaken my nerve.

A low, long screech from the hall told me that I had a man of uncommon brain to contend with, for I knew the sound came from his hands drawing along the banister, and that to husband his strength and to save time, he was sliding down. But this did not disconcert me. It pleased me. The quicker he went down, the oftener he would have to walk up.

For half an hour I played with him, giving him just time to get down to the foot of the stairs before I raised the silver, and just time to reach the top before I lowered it, and then I grew tired of the sport—for it was nothing else to me—and decided to finish him off. I was getting sleepy, but it was evident that the burglar was not, and I was a little afraid I might fall asleep and thus defeat myself. The burglar had that advantage because he was used to night work. So I quickened my movements a little. When the burglar slid down I gave him just time to see the silver rise through the ceiling, and when he climbed the stairs I only allowed him to see it descend through the floor. In this way I made him double his pace, and as I quickened my movements I soon had him dashing up the stairs and sliding down again as if for a wager. I did not give him a moment for rest, and he was soon panting terribly and beginning to stumble; but with almost superhuman nerve he kept up the chase. He was an unusually tough burglar.

But quick as he was I was always quicker, and a glimpse of the glowing case was all I let him have at either end of his climb or slide. No sooner was he down than it was up, and no sooner was the case up than he was up after it. In this way I kept increasing his speed until it was something terrific, and the whole house shook, like an automobile with a very powerful motor. But still his speed increased. I saw then that I had brought him to the place I had prepared for, where he had but one object in life, and that was to beat the case up or down stairs; and as I was now so sleepy I could hardly keep my eyes open, I did what I had intended to do from the first. I lowered the case until it was exactly between the ceiling of the dining-room and the floor of the hall above—and turned out the electric light. I then tied the steel cable securely to the head of my bed, turned over, and went to sleep, lulled by the shaking of the house as the burglar dashed up and down the stairs.

Just how long this continued I do not know, for my sleep was deep and dreamless, but I should judge that the burglar ran himself to death sometime between half-past three and a quarter after four.

So great had been his efforts that when I went to remove him I did not recognize him at all. When I had seen him last in the glow of the glass silver case he had been a stout, chunky fellow, and now his remains were those of an emaciated man. He must have run off one hundred and twenty pounds of flesh before he gave out.

Only one thing clouded my triumph. Our silver consisted of but half a dozen each of knives, forks, and spoons, a butter knife, and a sugar spoon, all plated, and worth probably five dollars, and to save this I had made the burglar wear to rags a Wilton stair carpet worth twenty-nine dollars. But I have now corrected this. I have bought fifty dollars worth of silver.